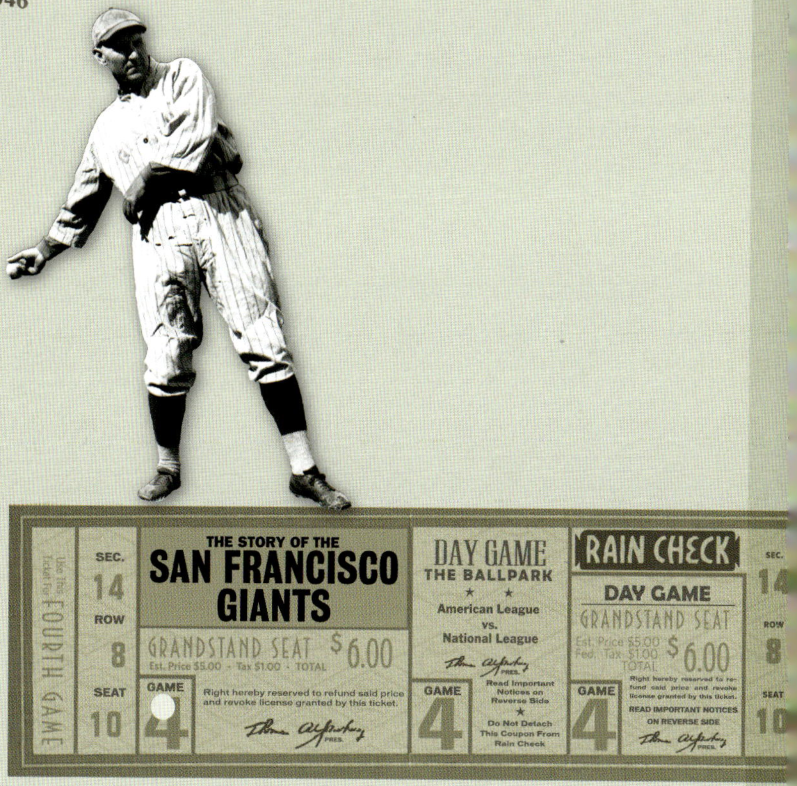
Use This Ticket For FOURTH GAME
SEC. 14
ROW 8
SEAT 10
THE STORY OF THE
SAN FRANCISCO GIANTS
GRANDSTAND SEAT $6.00
Est. Price $5.00 · Tax $1.00 · TOTAL
GAME 4
Right hereby reserved to refund said price and revoke license granted by this ticket.
DAY GAME
THE BALLPARK
American League vs. National League
GAME 4
Read Important Notices on Reverse Side
Do Not Detach This Coupon From Rain Check
RAIN CHECK
DAY GAME
GRANDSTAND SEAT
GAME 4
READ IMPORTANT NOTICES ON REVERSE SIDE

Published by Creative Education
P.O. Box 227, Mankato, Minnesota 56002
Creative Education is an imprint of The Creative Company

Design and production by Blue Design
Printed in the United States of America

Photographs by Corbis (Bettmann), Getty Images (APA, Brian Bahr, Bruce Bennett Studio, MONICA DAVEY/AFP, Dennis Desprois/MLB Photos, Diamond Images, Otto Greule Jr/Allsport, Otto Greule Jr/Stringer, JEFF HAYNES/AFP, Jed Jacobsohn, MPI, MLB Photos, National Baseball Hall of Fame Library/MLB Photos, Olen Collection/Diamond Images, Photo File/MLB Photos, Rich Pilling/MLB Photos, Robert Riger, Mark Rucker/Transcendental Graphics, Don Smith/MLB Photos, W. Eugene Smith//Time Life Pictures, Ron Vesely/MLB Photos), National Baseball Hall of Fame Library, Cooperstown, N.Y

Library of Congress Cataloging-in-Publication Data

Richardson, Adele, 1966-
The story of the San Francisco Giants / by Adele Richardson.
p. cm. — (Baseball: the great American game)
Includes index.
ISBN-13: 978-1-58341-499-6
1. San Francisco Giants (Baseball team)—History—Juvenile literature. I. Title. II. Series.

GV875.S34R53 2007
796.3570979461—dc22 2006028088

First Edition
9 8 7 6 5 4 3 2 1

Cover: Outfielder Willie Mays
Page 1: Pitcher Amos Rusie
Page 3: Pitcher Matt Cain

THE STORY OF THE

SAN FRANCISCO GIANTS

by Adele Richardson

BARRY BONDS

THE STORY OF THE

San Francisco Giants

Fans at Anaheim's Edison International Field are torn. It's October 19, 2002, and the first game of the World Series is heading into the second inning with no runs on the board. While they want their beloved home team, the Anaheim Angels, to best the San Francisco Giants, many in the crowd can't help but get goose bumps as record-breaking slugger Barry Bonds steps to the plate. Angels hurler Jarrod Washburn's third pitch is a straight fastball that the left fielder watches go by. The sharp-eyed Bonds is patient, just waiting for Washburn to make the slightest mistake. As the fourth pitch leaves Washburn's hand, Bonds sees that it's going to catch too much of the plate. He swings and connects. The crowd stands as one as the ball sails over the outfield wall. Bonds has just hit career home run number 610 and become the 26th player in history to go deep in his first World Series at bat.

GIGANTIC BEGINNINGS

When it was founded in 1776 as a small Spanish mission, no one dreamed that San Francisco would blossom into the thriving metropolis of more than 7.5 million that it is today. The San Francisco Bay area has been an attractive destination for more than two centuries. During the gold rush of the early 1800s, people were lured to the city by the promise of fortune. Although wealth was elusive to many, everyone could enjoy the area's natural beauty. One hundred years later, it was no great wonder that Major League Baseball also heard the call to "go west."

However, long before the Giants came to call San Francisco home, the team had already established itself as a winning franchise in New York City called the Gothams. In 1883, owner John B. Day's Gothams played their first game on a field that was once used for polo games. From then on, the field was known as the Polo Grounds.

ROGER CONNOR – Connor hit the first grand slam in major-league history (in 1881) and went on to become the most celebrated home run hitter of the 1800s. The huge (6-foot-3 and 220 pounds) first baseman played in a Giants uniform for 10 seasons.

ROGER CONNOR

BUCK EWING

BUCK EWING – Many baseball historians consider Ewing the finest all-around player of the 19th century. He could play any position, was always among the league batting leaders, led the NL in home runs (10) in 1883, and stole 53 bases during the 1888 season.

QUESTIONABLE ORIGINS

For its first two years of existence, the team that would be known one day as the San Francisco Giants was called the New York Gothams. Several people have claimed the honor of bestowing the new titanic name on the franchise, but the truth is lost to history. One story goes that on June 3, 1885, team manager Jim Mutrie was so overcome with emotion after his players earned an extra-inning win over the Philadelphia Phillies that he called out, "My Giants! My Giants!" The nickname stuck and soon became the official name of the team. Another story gives the credit to writer P.J. Donohue. During the 1885 season, the Gothams played phenomenal baseball. Two of their pitchers combined for 76 wins, and four players batted over .300. Third baseman Roger Connor, one of those four, hit an amazing .371 for the season. After watching the Gothams' remarkable play in the field and at the plate, Donohue began calling the team "Giants" whenever he referred to them. Of course, the name could have been coined by someone else entirely, or perhaps it stuck because of a combination of the two men's comments. Regardless, the team ended up with a big, new name in 1885.

Early Gothams stars were catcher Buck Ewing and first baseman Roger Connor, who both posted batting averages over .300 and carried the team with their powerful bats. Ewing was an immediate fan favorite because of his prowess behind and at the plate. His sense of humor was just as wicked as his arm. During one extra-inning game, an impatient (and apparently hungry) Ewing shouted to the crowd, "It's getting late. I'm going to steal home, and then we can all have dinner." A few pitches later, he did just that.

Changing its name to the Giants in 1885 didn't seem to have a measurable effect on the team, which, while not as successful in the 1890s as it had been in the 1880s, still had its bright spots: pitching sensation Amos Rusie posted 4 seasons in a row

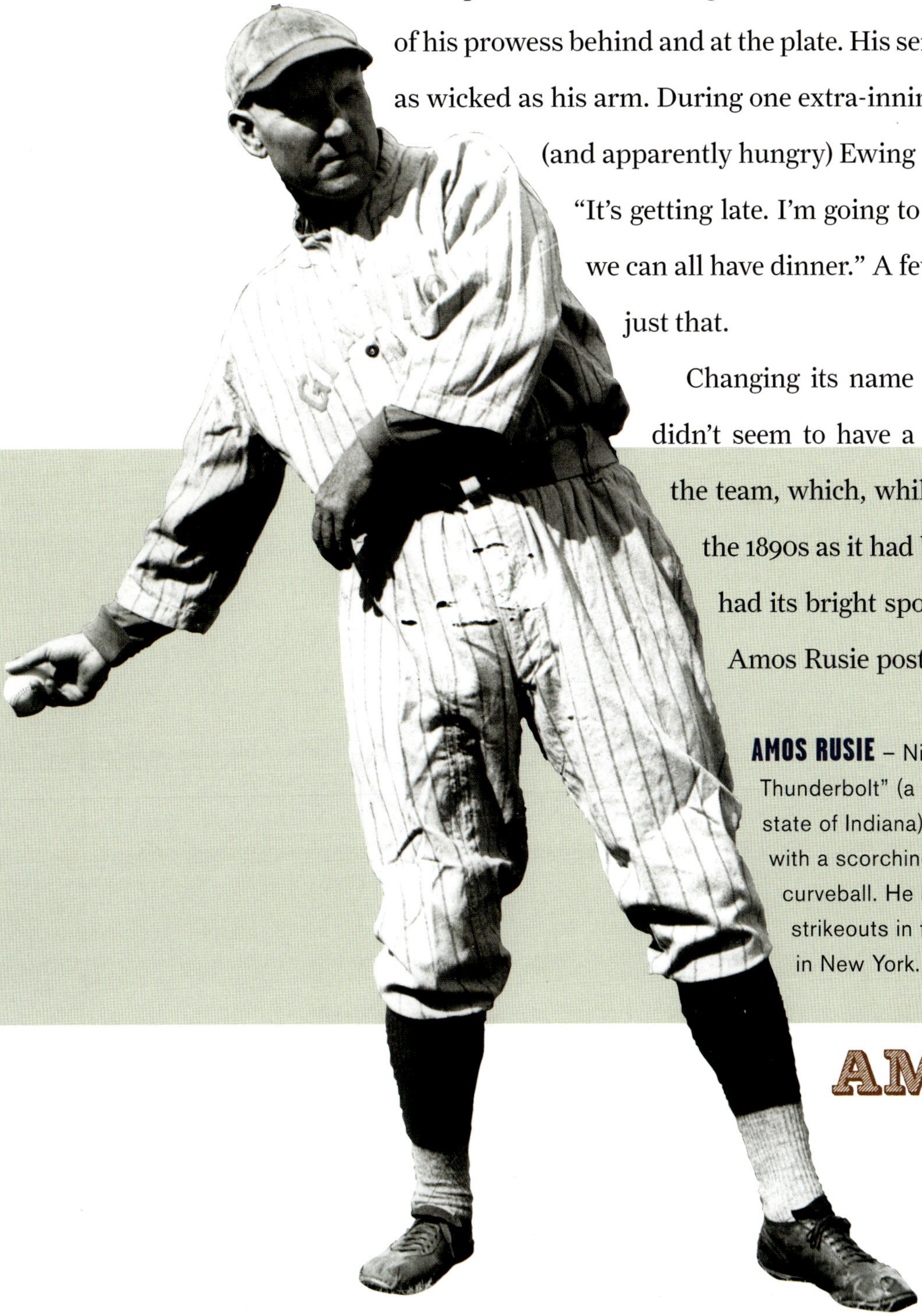

AMOS RUSIE – Nicknamed "The Hoosier Thunderbolt" (a reference to his home state of Indiana), Rusie befuddled hitters with a scorching fastball and masterful curveball. He led all NL pitchers in strikeouts in five of his eight seasons in New York.

AMOS RUSIE

with 31 or more wins, and shortstop George Davis led the offense by stealing base after base and keeping his batting average at a steady .300. Still, the team never placed better than second in the National League (NL) and, in 1899, sunk as low as 10th in the 12-team league. The situation for the Giants, and for all of major league baseball, changed drastically in 1902 when moody, hard-nosed infielder John McGraw took control of the team as player/manager.

ON THE ROAD TO GREATNESS

At the age of 29, McGraw was given the reins to the worst team in the NL. Although still young, his gruff, dictatorial manner earned him the nickname "Little Napoleon" and enabled him to lead the Giants to an eventual turnaround in the standings. "No club that wins a pennant once is an outstanding club," McGraw said. "One which bunches two pennants is a good club. But a team which can win three in a row really achieves greatness."

McGraw had his work cut out for him. The Giants hit a mere 8 home runs his first year, and the pitching staff rang up only 48 wins—14 of which were credited to Christy Mathewson. The next year, the Giants unexpectedly rock-

JOHN McGRAW

Known for his hard-driving, "win-at-all-costs" philosophy, John McGraw built the Giants into a powerhouse.

PITCHER · CHRISTY MATHEWSON

A powerful right-hander, "Matty" routinely tied batters in knots with his baffling fadeaway pitch. The Giants' all-time leader in shutouts, wins, complete games, strikeouts, and innings pitched, Mathewson posted 4 seasons with 30 or more wins during his career. Along with baseball greats Honus Wagner, Walter Johnson, Babe Ruth, and Ty Cobb, Mathewson was part of the initial induction class into the Hall of Fame. A college-educated man, Mathewson was also an accomplished checkers player, and he once beat world champion Newell Banks, who reigned as checkers king from 1917 to 1922 and from 1933 to 1934.

STATS

Giants seasons: 1900–16

Height: 6-2

Weight: 195

- **2,502 career strikeouts**
- **12 consecutive 20-win seasons**
- **2.13 career ERA**
- **Baseball Hall of Fame inductee (1936)**

eted up to second place, and finally, in 1904, the boys from New York brought home the NL pennant with a 106–47 record.

McGraw knew he had phenomenal talent at his disposal. Shortstop Bill Dahlen led the team with 80 runs batted in (RBI) in 1904, but the real power was on the mound. Joe "Iron Man" McGinnity, who earned his nickname because he never seemed to tire, won an outstanding 35 games that year. Mathewson, who was not far behind with 33, also mystified batters with his signature sweeping curveball. While many marveled at Mathewson's command, he was nonplussed about it, remarking, "Anybody's best pitch is the one batters ain't hitting that day."

But the pennant wasn't good enough for McGraw; he wanted a World Series title. In 1905, the Giants delivered. Each of the Giants' 5 pitchers threw for a minimum of 15 wins, and center fielder Mike Donlin was a terror at

THE MERKLE GAME

In 1908, the Giants and Chicago Cubs finished regular season play with identical records: 98–55. Because of the tie, the teams played one more game on September 23 to decide who would take home the NL pennant. With two outs in the bottom of the ninth inning and Giants runners at first and third base, shortstop Al Bridwell came to the plate and cracked the game-winning hit. Or so many people thought. Exuberant Giants fans stormed the field as soon as they realized Bridwell's swing was a hit. First baseman Fred Merkle, the Giants player who had been running from first base, thought the game was over and headed for the dugout, never touching second base. The quick-thinking Cubs found the ball and tagged second, prompting the umpires to call Merkle out. Between screaming fans and a riotous Giants dugout, order could not be restored on the field, and the umps ended up declaring the game a 1–1 tie. Because of Merkle's mistake, the game became known as "Merkle's Game." The teams met again on October 8 for another tiebreaker, and the Giants lost 4–2. The Cubs went on to take the pennant and the World Series.

the plate, hitting .356 with seven homers. With such a combination of dominant pitching and clutch hitting, the Giants won another pennant and then brought home a world championship by beating the Philadelphia Athletics four games to one in the World Series.

Over the next few years, New York became the home of baseball's elite, as the Giants won three straight NL pennants in 1911, 1912, and 1913. The Giants' success continued into the early 1920s, and among the talented crew were outfielder Irish Meusel, first baseman George Kelly, and second baseman Frankie Frisch. The Giants won an additional four straight NL pennants and two World Series (1921 and 1922). McGraw was poised to achieve immortality by leading his club to three titles in a row, but the New York Yankees topped the Giants in the 1923 World Series.

After winning the 1924 NL pennant but losing the World Series to the Washington Senators, the Giants began to slide in the standings, never placing better than second. By the time McGraw retired in 1932, the Giants were in sixth place, but McGraw had become one of the winningest and longest-serving managers in baseball history. In 31 seasons, he had earned 10 NL pennants, 3 World Series championships, and the respect of countless players, fans, and fellow managers.

JOE McGINNITY

Joe McGinnity was nicknamed "Iron Man" partly because he worked in a metal-making factory in the off-season.

MEL OTT

CHANGING OF THE GUARD

When first baseman Bill Terry took over as manager midway through the 1932 season, he had some big-name players to work with. Right fielder Mel Ott was hitting long balls left and right with his odd "foot-in-the-bucket" step, so named because, as the pitch approached, he lifted his right foot as if he were stepping into a bucket. And pitcher "King Carl" Hubbell topped the 100-strikeout mark for the fourth year in a row. The Giants couldn't pull it together in 1932, but in 1933, they made it all the way to the World Series and won it—beating the Senators—thanks to their outstanding pitching staff. Hubbell and Hal Schumacher threw a combined 17 shutouts that year, with King Carl throwing 46 and a half consecutive shutout innings.

Under Terry's guidance, the Giants battled hard over the next two years to finish in second and third place. In 1936, they won the NL pennant and faced off against the New York Yankees in the World Series. After allowing the Yankees to score only one run during Game 1, Hubbell accidentally hit Yankees slugger Lou Gehrig in the eighth inning, and with the bat taken out of Gehrig's hands, the Giants went on to win. "I slipped, and the ball got away from

Mel Ott generated enormous power from his 170-pound frame, helping carry the Giants to three World Series.

CATCHER • BUCK EWING

A terror behind the plate, William "Buck" Ewing's cannon arm could throw out would-be base stealers even while he remained in his catcher's crouch. With a bat in his hand, he was just as deadly. In his rookie year, Ewing hit three triples in one game and became the first major-league player ever to hit 10 home runs in a season. He hit .300 or better in 10 of his 15 years in the majors, and in 1900 he co-managed the Giants with shortstop George Davis. Ewing was considered a "complete" ballplayer, also logging time at first base, in the outfield, and on the pitcher's mound.

STATS

Giants seasons: 1883–92

Height: 5-10

Weight: 188

- **1,625 career hits**
- **.303 career BA**
- **354 career stolen bases**
- **Baseball Hall of Fame inductee (1939)**

me with nothing on it," Hubbell explained. "Maybe it's lucky it hit Lou, instead of going over the plate." The Yankees retaliated in Game 2, battering the Giants, 18–4, and eventually won the series four games to two.

The Giants made another run to the "Fall Classic" in 1937 but were once again stumped by the Yankees. The team lagged in the standings for the next three years and finished in sixth place in 1940. In 1942, Mel Ott took over as manager, and power-hitting first baseman Johnny Mize was acquired from the St. Louis Cardinals. But the Giants still couldn't finish better than third place. One reason was that World War II was underway and many ballclubs were losing players to the military. The Giants were particularly hard-hit; Mize and several others were called up to serve in 1943, and Mize would not return until 1946.

Ott's third-place 1942 club would be his best as manager. He left the helm in 1948, and in a move that stunned everyone, Giants brass brought in manager Leo Durocher from the archrival Brooklyn Dodgers to finish out the season. Just two years before, the scrappy Durocher had coined the phrase "Nice guys finish last." Now he would be given the chance to bring the "nice guy" Giants out of their post-war slump and back into World Series contention.

Johnny Mize returned from World War II service better than ever, putting up 51 homers and 138 RBI in 1947.

JOHNNY MIZE

"SAY HEY" SAN FRANCISCO

Even with the demanding Durocher at the helm, the Giants couldn't break out of their slump until 1951, when a late-season winning streak forced a three-game playoff series with the Brooklyn Dodgers for the NL pennant. The dramatic series went down to the bottom of the ninth inning of Game 3 with the score 4–2. Then, Giants third baseman Bobby Thomson crushed a game-winning, three-run homer that is still considered one of the most famous at bats in baseball history.

On deck to witness Thomson's "Shot Heard 'Round the World" was rookie center fielder Willie Mays. Although Mays missed the next two seasons while serving in the Korean War, he returned to lead the Giants to another World Series run in 1954. Their adversaries, the Cleveland Indians, were heavily favored to win, but Mays had other ideas. In Game 1, with the score tied 2–2 in the eighth and two Cleveland runners on base, Indians power-hitting first baseman Vic Wertz belted the ball to the deepest part of center field. Nearly everyone thought it was going to go over Mays's head, but the graceful center fielder reached up, made an amazing over-the-shoulder catch, then slung the ball back to the infield, holding both runners in place. The play,

WILLIE MAYS

WILLIE MAYS – The "Say Hey Kid" quickly became a legend. He was a New York folk hero, an All-Star every year from 1954 to 1973, and his sprinting catch, spin, and throw in the 1954 World Series remains one of baseball's most famous plays.

THOMSON'S SHOT

Down by 13 and a half games in the NL standings by mid-August, things weren't looking good for the 1951 Giants. But then the team went on an improbable streak, winning 16 consecutive games and 37 of its final 44. The feat led to a best-of-three playoff series for the pennant against the Giants' rival, the Brooklyn Dodgers. Having each won one game apiece, the teams headed into Game 3. In the ninth inning of Game 3, the Giants were in their final at bat and down 4–2. With two Giants players on base, Dodgers hurler Ralph Branca threw a strike on the outside corner to Giants third baseman Bobby Thomson. The second pitch was up and inside. The third toss was a breaking ball, down and away—a bad pitch that Thomson swung at anyway. Thomson miraculously connected and yanked the ball down the left-field line. The ball kept sailing until it dropped into the stands just over the fence. The homer, which not only won the Giants the game but the NL pennant as well, is remembered as "The Shot Heard 'Round the World" and marked one of the most dramatic playoff moments in baseball history.

known simply as "The Catch," took the wind out of the Indians' sails, and the Giants snatched up another World Series title in four games.

Given the nickname the "Say Hey Kid" for his friendly habit of saying "say hey, man," to players whose names he didn't know, Mays quickly became one of the most popular players in the dugout and in the stands. Durocher knew he had a special star on his hands right away. "He could do the five things you have to do to be a superstar: hit, hit with power, run, throw, and field," the skipper marveled. "And he had that other ingredient that turns a superstar into a super superstar. He lit up the room when he came in. He was a joy to be around."

Despite the Kid's efforts, attendance waned at New York's Polo Grounds, prompting the Giants to move across the country to San Francisco in 1958. As the Giants made themselves at home in Seals Stadium, they welcomed several new players. Rookie Felipe Alou manned the outfield with Mays, and newcomer Orlando Cepeda took his place at first base.

In 1959, the roster was shuffled so that rookie Willie McCovey could take over at first, and another rookie, pitching sensation Juan Marichal, debuted in 1960. That same year, the Giants moved into Candlestick Park on the western shore of San Francisco Bay, where the swirling winds in the outfield often wreaked havoc on fly balls. When future Hall of Fame pitcher Gaylord Perry was added in 1962, the Giants surged to the pennant with a 103–62

FIRST BASEMAN · WILLIE McCOVEY

Willie "Stretch" McCovey exploded onto the big-league scene in 1959, as his .354 batting average and winsome personality earned him the NL Rookie of the Year award. McCovey's sweeping swing was the envy of the majors, and he racked up more than 500 dingers and 2,200 hits throughout his career. He was given a permanent place of honor at the Giants' modern home stadium when McCovey Cove, the waters behind the right-field wall of AT&T Park, was named after him. McCovey's number 44 uniform, which he wore in honor of fellow Alabamian and home run king Hank Aaron, was retired by the Giants in 1981.

STATS

Giants seasons: 1959–73, 1977–80

Height: 6-4

Weight: 210

- **6-time All-Star**
- **18 career grand slams**
- **521 career HR**
- **Baseball Hall of Fame inductee (1986)**

mark. Although San Francisco battled for seven games in the World Series, the trophy went back east with its old rivals, the Yankees.

The team spent the rest of the 1960s finishing no higher than second place. But during those seasons, Mays still thrilled the fans with his booming bat and slick fielding, and Mike McCormick won the first Cy Young Award (as the league's best pitcher) by a Giants hurler with his 150 strikeouts in 1967. McCovey also slugged more than 30 round-trippers per season from 1965 through 1970, including a career-high 45 in 1969, the year the NL split into two divisions, placing San Francisco in the NL Western Division.

JUAN MARICHAL

JUAN MARICHAL – Marichal combined a strange, high-kicking delivery with an assortment of pitches to become a star. More infamously, he is remembered by some for his part in a particularly nasty on-field brawl between the Giants and Dodgers in 1965.

DIFFERENT COAST, SAME STORY

Just four years after moving to San Francisco, the Giants found themselves facing off against their old rivals, the New York Yankees, in the 1962 World Series. The first six games produced alternating wins, but the first four innings of Game 7 produced nothing. The Yanks managed to put a run on the board in the fifth, but the Giants' pitching staff refused to relinquish any more. The bottom of the ninth was do-or-die for San Francisco. Giants outfielder Matty Alou led off the inning with a pinch-hit bunt. Yankees hurler Ralph Terry next struck out Alou's brother and fellow outfielder Felipe, as well as second baseman Chuck Hiller. Alou was still stranded at first as center fielder Willie Mays stepped to the plate. The "Say Hey Kid" made the crowd say "hey" when he belted a double to right field, but Yankees outfielder Roger Maris chased down the ball and fired it to third, preventing Alou from scoring. When Willie McCovey came to bat, the tension was thick in Candlestick Park. With a 1–1 count, McCovey hit a hard liner, but Yankees second baseman Bobby Richardson leaped to snag the final out, giving New York its 20th World Series title and taking a world championship from the Giants for the fifth time.

ALL-TIME TEAM

SECOND BASEMAN · JEFF KENT

Jeff Kent never settled for less than his best—perhaps that was why he made it to the postseason six times over the course of his career. The intense second-sacker had a banner season in 2000, when he assembled a career-high .334 batting average and won the NL MVP award. Although Kent was known to squabble with his teammates on occasion, he could always be relied on to perform at the plate. While in San Francisco, Kent contributed more than 100 RBI each season and even hit for the rare cycle on May 3, 1999, hitting a single, double, triple, and home run against the Pittsburgh Pirates.

STATS

Giants seasons: 1997–2002

Height: 6-1

Weight: 205

- **5-time All-Star**
- **2,189 career hits**
- **1,380 career RBI**
- **501 career doubles**

ALL-TIME TEAM

THIRD BASEMAN · DARRELL EVANS

Pitchers knew better than to give Darrell Evans good pitches to swing at; in 1976, he was walked in 15 consecutive games. Yet Evans still became the first player in major-league history to hit 40 or more homers in a season in both the American League (AL) and the NL. Hitting a home run was the best feeling in the world for Evans. "It's what you live for. Sometimes it is what you die for," he said. "You put one up there and it makes you feel young again." Evans was one of only three players ever to belt 400 or more career homers and not make the Baseball Hall of Fame.

STATS

Giants seasons: 1976–83

Height: 6-2

Weight: 205

- **2,223 career hits**
- **2-time All-Star**
- **1,605 career walks**
- **414 career HR**

YOUNG AND OLD

Six weeks into the 1970 season, the Giants hired former catcher Charlie Fox as manager. Fox led the team to a third-place finish that year, but 1971 became known as the "Year of the Fox." That season, the Giants started out 18–5 and never looked back. When they faced off against the Pittsburgh Pirates in the NL Championship Series (NLCS), the Giants thought they had it in the bag; they had already beaten the Pirates 9 out of 12 games in regular-season play. Pittsburgh, however, had a postseason burst of energy and took the series three games to one, despite a McCovey three-run homer in Game 4. "It just goes to show you that anything can happen in the playoffs," San Francisco's star first baseman said.

During the next 15 years, the Giants exhibited their share of highlights. Shortstop Chris Speier and second baseman Tito Fuentes turned over one dynamic double play after another during these years. And in 1973, outfielder Bobby Bonds missed becoming baseball's first player to hit 40 home runs and steal 40 bases in a season by only one home run. Still, the team hovered between third and sixth place in the standings.

New players appeared year after year in the dugout, while old favorites parted ways. Marichal and McCovey both left in 1973, to the disappointment of the San Francisco faithful. McCovey would return in 1977, but while he was gone, Darrell Evans was acquired to take over at first base. Pitchers, fearing his bat, often aimed outside the strike zone, allowing Evans to set an NL record in 1976 by being walked in 15 consecutive games. In 1981, the team made headlines when baseball legend Frank Robinson took the helm, becoming the first African American manager in the NL. But even Robinson's immense knowledge and experience couldn't pull San Francisco up in the standings, and he left partway through his fourth year.

BOBBY BONDS

BOBBY BONDS – Bonds brought to San Francisco the same muscular physique (and uniform number) for which his son Barry would later be known. The elder Bonds was hailed for his slugging power and captured three Gold Gloves for his great outfield play.

SHORTSTOP · GEORGE DAVIS

Being an extraordinary fielder, batter, and base runner was all in a day's work for George Davis. During his 20 years in the majors, the switch hitter batted over .300 in 9 seasons. And once he got on base, he'd steal the next one if a pitcher didn't pay close attention. In 1893, his first year in New York, Davis's play was inspiring. He not only built a then-record 33-game hitting streak, but he also became the first player in history to whack a triple and a homer in the same inning. Known for his craftiness and baseball knowledge, Davis played 1895, 1900, and 1901 as co-manager of the Giants.

STATS

Giants seasons: 1893–1901, 1903

Height: 5-9

Weight: 180

- **2,660 career hits**
- **616 career stolen bases**
- **.295 career BA**
- **Baseball Hall of Fame inductee (1998)**

ALL-TIME TEAM

LEFT FIELDER · BARRY BONDS

If anyone had baseball in his blood, it was Barry Bonds. The son of major-league outfielder Bobby Bonds and godson of center fielder Willie Mays, it's no wonder that Barry became a seven-time NL MVP. The 13-time All-Star belted a homer in his first at bat of the 2002 World Series, and he broke more long-standing records than any other player. By 2003, he had become the only player in history to achieve 500 homers and 500 stolen bases, and in 2006, Bonds slugged home run number 715, putting him ahead of Babe Ruth and in second place on baseball's all-time home run list. He had 734 homers by the end of 2006.

STATS

Giants seasons: 1993–present

Height: 6-2

Weight: 228

- **8-time Gold Glove winner**
- **73 home runs in 2001 (most all-time)**
- **2,152 career runs scored**
- **1,930 career RBI**

JACK CLARK

THE NINE-DAY GAME

When the Giants played the Chicago Cubs on July 20, 1978, it was San Francisco's last scheduled trip to Wrigley Field for the season. The Cubs got on the board first by scoring two runs in the first inning. The two teams battled back and forth, and by the end of the seventh inning, the game was tied 8–8. In the first half of the eighth inning, the Giants managed a single, a sacrifice bunt, and a ground out before right fielder Jack Clark singled to left, giving San Francisco a 9–8 lead. But the game, which started at 3:16 P.M., was running a little long. When the Giants scored their ninth run in the eighth inning, it was 6:34 P.M. And it was getting dark. Since Wrigley did not have outside lighting, the game was suspended until the next time the two teams met. So on July 28, 1978, the Giants and Cubs set up shop again, this time in San Francisco's Candlestick Park. They picked up right where they had left off, down to the same lineups. Neither team scored during the remaining 10 outs, and the Giants ended up with baseball's most drawn-out win ever.

WILL CLARK

After Robinson's departure, the 1985 season became the worst ever for the Giants. After plunging to last place in the NL West for the second year in a row, insult was added to injury when the Giants finished the year with the only 100-loss season in their history. Roger Craig, a former pitcher who was known for his blistering split-finger fastball, came aboard as manager with every intention of turning things around. Rookie first baseman Will "The Thrill" Clark also joined the team in 1986 and made headlines by blasting a homer in his first at bat.

Rookies and veterans melded their talents with stunning success the next year, propelling the team to another division championship in 1987. Two years later, the Giants went 92–70 and made it back to the World Series, where they faced the Oakland Athletics for the first-ever Bay Area World Series. The Giants lost the first two games but were confident heading into Game 3. However, just half an hour before the game was scheduled to start, a major earthquake rocked the Bay Area, damaging Candlestick Park and postponing the game for 10 days. The Giants never recovered, losing the series in four games.

ALL-TIME TEAM

CENTER FIELDER • WILLIE MAYS

The "Say Hey Kid," Willie Mays, was the original "five-tool" player according to manager Leo Durocher—he could do everything, and he did everything well. The 1951 Rookie of the Year was a 2-time NL MVP and earned 12 Gold Gloves as the league's best center fielder. Mays was the first player ever to hit 50 homers and steal 30 bases in a season, and he was also one of only four players ever to collect 500 homers and 3,000 hits. The man widely regarded as one of the best ballplayers in history was honored when the Giants retired his uniform number (24) soon after Mays hung up his glove.

STATS

Giants seasons: 1951–72

Height: 5-11

Weight: 180

- **3,283 career hits**
- **20-time All-Star**
- **2,062 career runs scored**
- **Baseball Hall of Fame inductee (1979)**

ETERNAL CONTENDERS

At the end of the 1992 season, the Giants were nearly at the bottom of the division—26 games out of first. The franchise then brought in manager Dusty Baker and left fielder Barry Bonds to wake the sleeping Giants in 1993. The additions paid off immediately, as the new-look team soared to second place. For his efforts, Baker took home the NL Manager of the Year award.

Much of the credit also went to Bonds, a two-time league Most Valuable Player (MVP) who had earned renown for his cannon arm in the outfield before joining the Giants. In his first year with the team, he also showcased his awesome offensive skills by swiping 29 bases, jacking 46 homers, and driving in 123 runs. With the help of pitchers John Burkett and Bill Swift, who each logged more than 20 wins, the team reestablished itself as an NL power.

Baker kept the team near the top of the standings for much of the 1990s. When Giants brass added the bats of second baseman Jeff Kent and first baseman J.T. Snow in 1997, San Francisco earned another trip to the postseason. The young Florida Marlins proved to be too much, though, knocking the Giants out of the playoffs.

After two second-place seasons, the Giants sought a fresh beginning in 2000 when they moved into the new Pacific Bell Park. Unfortunately, the

RIGHT FIELDER • MEL OTT

"Master Melvin" was a fan favorite during his 22 years with the Giants. Coming to the organization in 1926 as a scrawny 17-year-old, Ott's unusual style of lifting his right foot before smashing his bat into the pitch amazed fans and opponents alike with its effectiveness—it always seemed as if he would miss the ball entirely. Ott was the first NL player to rack up 500 home runs and recorded 8 years with 30 or more dingers. Twice in his career he was walked six times in a double-header. From 1942 to 1948, Ott also managed the team (continuing for a year after he stopped playing).

STATS

Giants seasons: 1926–47 (1948 as manager)

Height: 5-9

Weight: 170

- **12-time All-Star**
- **511 career HR**
- **.304 career BA**
- **Baseball Hall of Fame inductee (1951)**

J.T. SNOW

J.T. SNOW – The son of former professional football player Jack Snow, J.T. earned a reputation as the slickest-fielding first baseman in the NL in the late '90s. He also was a valuable RBI man, driving home 104 runs to help the 1997 Giants win the NL West.

GIANTS
neweraca
neweraca
Bank of Ame

Barry Bonds won the fourth of seven career NL MVP awards with his record-shattering 73 homers in 2001.

BARRY BONDS

RAY DURHAM

A former Chicago White Sox star, second baseman Ray Durham helped San Francisco win 100 games in 2003.

team christened the park with six straight losses. But the Giants had been around long enough that fans and opponents knew better than to count them out. A late-season streak landed the team in first place in the NL West with a 97–65 mark, earning the Giants a playoff date with the New York Mets. The Mets put an end to the magic, though, winning the series in four games.

In 2001, Bonds put on the show of shows, slamming 73 homers and breaking St. Louis Cardinals slugger Mark McGwire's single-season home run record of 70. More amazing was that he did it despite being walked a major-league record 177 times. "This was one of the greatest years—no, it was *the* greatest year—I have seen from a single person," marveled Baker.

Bonds' 46 homers in 2002 helped propel the team to an NL Wild Card berth.

ALL-TIME TEAM

MANAGER • JOHN McGRAW

The demanding man known as "Little Napoleon" became the winningest manager in Giants history and the second-winningest manager in baseball history. During McGraw's lengthy tenure, the Giants finished in first or second place 20 times. He was integral in developing several strategic plays that managers still use, such as the hit-and-run and the squeeze play (in which the batter bunts so that the runner on third base can score). During his first five years with the Giants, McGraw was also a player, spending time primarily at shortstop. McGraw's uniform, even though it had no number, is recognized as "retired" by the franchise.

STATS

Giants seasons as manager: 1902–32

Height: 5-7

Weight: 155

Managerial Record: 2,763–1,948

World Series Championships: 1905, 1921, 1922

WHAT GOES AROUND . . .

Fate has a way of getting in the last word when teams resort to getting cheap outs with the old hidden ball trick. San Francisco has been on both sides of this sleight-of-hand issue. On June 28, 1994, the Giants were hosting the Los Angeles Dodgers. In the sixth inning, Dodgers shortstop Rafael Bournigal slammed a triple, barely beating the throw to third. Within seconds of catching the ball, Giants third baseman Matt Williams (who still had the "in play" ball), asked the rookie to step off so he could clean the base. And Bournigal did it! The Giants got the out they wanted, but they also lost the game 7–4. One year later, the Giants were playing the Colorado Rockies at Coors Field in Denver. In the first inning, Giants outfielder Darren Lewis was at third with left fielder Barry Bonds coming to the plate. Colorado third baseman Vinny Castilla tried his luck with the trick—and it worked. Lewis was tagged out, and the inning was over. Colorado should have learned from the Giants' trickery the year before: the game went into extra innings, and San Francisco pulled out a 2–1 win in the 11th.

After defeating the Atlanta Braves and St. Louis Cardinals, the Giants met the Anaheim Angels in the World Series. The Giants pushed the series to a deciding Game 7, but the Angels finally overpowered them to take home the title.

Fans' disappointment with the Fall Classic loss was compounded when Baker left to manage the Chicago Cubs. Team owners brought in former Giants outfielder Felipe Alou as a replacement, and he promptly led the team to another NL West title in 2003. Bonds continued to make headlines in 2004, earning his fourth-straight NL MVP award and hitting 45 home runs for the second year in a row, bringing his career total to 703. And even though the 2005 and 2006 seasons ended in losing records, Giants fans continued filling newly renamed AT&T Park to watch Bonds's pursuit of the all-time home run record and shortstop Omar Vizquel's brilliant fielding. The San Francisco faithful hoped that two key additions before the 2007 season—new manager Bruce Bochy and All-Star pitcher Barry Zito—would give the Giants the spark they needed to turn things back around.

For more than a century, the Giants have risen above adversity, whether on the East Coast or West, to provide their fans with exciting baseball. They have claimed 5 World Series trophies and have had 28 players inducted into the Hall of Fame. In the decades to come, those numbers are sure to rise, and fans look forward to the day the Giants will bring another championship home to the golden city of San Francisco.

INDEX